BAT
IN THE DINING ROOM

BY **CRESCENT DRAGONWAGON**
ILLUSTRATED BY **S. D. SCHINDLER**

MARSHALL CAVENDISH   **NEW YORK**

Text copyright © 1997 by Crescent Dragonwagon Illustrations © 1997 by S. D. Schindler
All rights reserved
Marshall Cavendish, 99 White Plains Road, Tarrytown, New York 10591
The text of this book is set in 14 point Stempel Schneidler
The illustrations are rendered in colored pencil and watercolor on pastel paper
Printed in Italy   First Marshall Cavendish Paperbacks Edition 2003
6 5 4 3 2 1
Library of Congress Cataloging-in-Publication Data
Dragonwagon, Crescent. Bat in the dining room / Crescent Dragonwagon; illustrated by S. D. Schindler   p. cm.
Summary: When a bat flies into a hotel restaurant, Melissa comes to the rescue.
ISBN 0-7614-5146-3 [1. Bats—Fiction. 2. Stories in rhyme] I Schindler, S. D., ill. II. Title.
PZ8.3.D77Bat 1997 [E]—dc21   96-54894   CIP AC

For Louis and Elsie Freund, who continue to open doors and encourage flight.
Love, C. D.

To Jim, McKey, Philip, Nellie, Winston, and Claire—good sports and bat friendly
S. D. S.

A bat flew into the dining room,
at the hotel restaurant by the lake.
Mistake.

The open window
must have called to it,
called it away
from sail and flit
from bat wings
from bat things
in from outside
from above the lake.
Mistake,
that bat in the hotel dining room.

Perhaps it fell?
No way to tell, or if it flew
down the chimney:
no one knew.
But suddenly, suddenly,
in the warm night air
in the hotel dining room
it was there
just a bat
confused and scared.

For a moment no one noticed it or saw
it circling wildly:
The ceiling high, the fans a-twirl,
the mothers fathers aunts and uncles
boys and girls—
cousins in-laws sisters brothers
Melissa, quiet, with the others
Waiters in their black and whites
summer evening, coming night.
Menus murmurs conversation
ordinary June vacation
"I think I'll start with the … fruit cup."
who would have even thought, "look up"?
Then someone did.

A woman in a large green hat
looked up and saw it and screamed "Bat!"
and ducked and screamed again, then more—

"A bat a bat a bat!"—the door
was rushed by panicked families
who crouched and gazed up frightenedly
covering heads with sunburnt arms
as if that bat could do them harm,
the babies bursting into tears
at all the screaming clutching fears
of parents cousins uncles aunts—
like that the dining room was cleared,
the patrons in the lobby.

Well! I never!
Did you ever!
Was it hiding in the curtains?
We're never coming *here* again, that's certain!
Ugh! I hate bats worse than anything—
It could have gotten in my hair!
Tell me, is it still in there?

But all that running for the door
and screaming just confused the bat still more

In vain the maître d' cried, "Please!
don't be alarmed, I have no doubt
in just a moment we'll have it out,
and dinner on the house."

Is there no one anywhere who guesses
how that thing which panicked them might be,
that dark gray bat shape, delicate,
frightened, circling crazily?
And could they ever, even one, think to feel
that bat's bat-fright,
spinning spinning spinning from outside, trapped
inside a strange enclosed and lit-up night?
Not even one in sympathy?
Yes. Melissa.
No one saw her yet.

The waiters and the chef talk loudly
in the kitchen by the dining room.
"Well, look, if I get a ladder, and a broom—"
"If we could stun it, catch it—"
"If we open all the windows wide—"
"Let's think, what else could we try?"

And bat, poor bat, its pitch too high
for anyone to hear, but in its panicked flight,
if anyone had looked and really seen
they could have heard (from just the way it moved),
a terrified cry
and seen its beautiful ridged wings beating like a heart
fluttering like moths . . .
where is it, how can it get out, how
did it get caught?

It wants its home night sky
no horizon chopped by roof and fan
just darkening air above and clear.

The bat careens into a fan blade and is stunned
and plummets to the floor
as conversation raises to a fever pitch
beyond the dining room door.
A boy peeking through the lobby glass, saw it, said
"It fell, it fell, oh good, I think it's dead!"

But Melissa hadn't run, she'd dropped to the floor,
under the table, cloth-draped in white,
watching, listening with all her might.
Strange Melissa, at school they called her weird,
that night she lifted up the tablecloth and peered:
and saw the bat, stunned, flapping on the floor
and she alone thought how the bat might feel.

And so she crept across the carpeted floor
and reached the outside exit door.
The others, panicked, had forgotten it.
Melissa knew, since only just that morning
she had noticed that outside door, exploring,
when she'd gone out herself, walking.

She loved her family, yes, but all that talking:
Mandy, her sister, Charles, her brother,
Mama, Daddy, Fred, the noisy others—
no quiet, not enough sometimes to think a single thought
sometimes Melissa just took off, escaped that feeling caught.

On her morning walk she'd seen that door,
just as she'd noticed, quiet, a thousand things or more.
A cardinal on a telephone wire
that the third swing on the left was higher
a padlocked gate, some lichen on a stone
a high-up bird's nest, which she left alone
the way the frogs got silent by the lake
when she walked close; and that the water
was more gray than blue
a thousand things that I or you
might not notice, might not see,
Melissa saw that morning, including
the dining room's outside exit door.

Was this seeing why Melissa knew that
the one most frightened of it all was the bat?

Her mother, in the lobby, just then missed her.
"Mandy! Where's Melissa, where's your sister!"
And as Melissa crawled out from beneath the table,
the bat began to fly again, since it was able.
"Ah, it's not dead, let's shoot it!" cried the watching boy,
seeing the bat, then added "Hey, there's a girl still there,
look at that, a girl in there, with that bat!"

"Melissa!" screamed her mother
racing for the lobby door,
"If I've told that child once, it's been
a thousand times or more—"
But before she could go in, Melissa reached
that secret door.

The door had a sign lit up in red:
emergency exit only, it said.
Melissa stood and pushed it, stepped outside
and held it open. "Come on, bat!" she cried,
but very softly, no one could hear.
"Come on bat, come on bat, come on out here!"

The bat continued circling in the dining room.
The chef was waiting, with a broom.
The maître d' was calling Department of Wildlife,
the little boy said, "Shoot it! Hit it! Throw a knife!"
But Melissa crouched there in the dark, kept saying
"Come on, bat,"

and with each circle the bat came closer
as if it smelled the soft night air
as if it saw the outside dark
as if it hoped but didn't dare
believe it might find its way again
back out of there
to dream of circling, darkling night
to lift bat-wings to be bat-right
to swoop and glide above the lake
to leave this strange enclosed mistake.

The wildlife officer had a gun
it would not kill but only stun
he drove up in his truck, he parked

but even then the bat moved there—
towards that piece of dark, a square
Melissa's opened door the way
the bat could fly out free, away,
and swoop out into nighttime.

"Come on, bat!", Melissa said
and then the bat flew out, above her head
her chin turned up, she saw it for an instant
a moving breeze of joy against the sky, and she smiled
and said, "Good-bye."

An hour later, all was calm,
dinner served to all guests, free,
and everyone discussed the bat excitedly,
and how brave the little girl'd been.

They fussed over Melissa,
called her kind to animals, and smart:
but no one had a clue
no one even knew
what was in her heart.
She smiled politely and said "Thank you very much,"
And "All I did was open up a door,"
And "I just remembered that exit from before."

But that night, when she crawled into bed
Melissa remembered, smiling in the dark,
the joyful moment when the bat
flew out and free above her head
and thought of it a-swoop a-glide
its panic ended, flit and soar
and that she'd held the open door;
now in its night, bat-circling and bat-limber
and thought, "I hope that bat's forgotten
this night, which I will always remember."